Hunches in Bunches

in

By

Dr. Seuss

RANDOM HOUSE 🏠 NEW YORK

Library of Congress Cataloging-in-Publication Data: Seuss, Dr. Hunches in bunches. SUMMARY: A boy has a difficult time making decisions even though there is a vocal bunch of Hunches to help him. [1. Stories in rhyme. 2. Decision making—Fiction] I. Title. PZ8.3.G276Hu 1982 [Fic] 82-50629 AACR2 ISBN: 0-394-85502-7 (trade); 0-394-95502-1 (lib. bdg.)

Manufactured in the United States of America   20 19 18 17 16 15 14 13

Do you ever sit and fidget
when you don't know what to do…?
Everybody gets the fidgets.
Even me and even you.
And today was quite an awful day
for me and my poor pup.

My trouble was I had a mind.
But I couldn't make it up.

It's awfully awfully awful
when you can't make up your mind!

Do you want to kick a football?
Or sit there on your behind?
Do you want to go out skating?
Fly a kite? Or climb a tree?
Do you want to eat a pizza?
Take a bath? Or watch TV?

Oh, you get so many hunches
that you don't know ever quite
if the right hunch is a wrong hunch!
Then the wrong hunch might be right!

There I was, inside the house,
so fuddled up I could shout,
when I got a hunch,
a Happy Hunch,
that I shouldn't be *in*...but OUT!

But before I could follow
that Happy Hunch,
a voice snapped,
"Don't you dare!"

And a Real Tough Hunch informed me,
"You're not going ANYwhere!
There is homework to be done, Bub!
Sit your pants down on that chair!"

And so I did. I sat me down.
But as soon as I got sat,
a Better Hunch came
and he yanked off
the Homework Hunch's hat.

The Better Hunch said, "We'll head downtown.
We'll pick up your good friend James
and together we'll trot to some real cool spot
and we'll play a few video games!"

So, of course, that's what I started to do,
but a Sour Hunch came to spoil it.
"Your bicycle's rusting up!" he yapped.
"Get yourself out back and oil it!"

By now my mind was *so* mixed up
I really didn't know
if I wanted to go to the barber shop
or to Boise, Idaho.

Then a Very Odd Hunch upset me
when he asked me loud and clear,
"Do you think it might be helpful
if you went to the bathroom, dear?"

Before I could even answer him,
a new voice interrupted.
"That mind of yours," I heard him say,
"is frightfully ga-fluppted.
Your mind is murky-mooshy!
Will you make it up? Or won't you?
If you won't, you are a wonter!
Do you understand? Or don't you?
If you don't, you are a donter.
You're a canter if you can't.
I would really like to help you.
But you're hopeless. So I shan't."

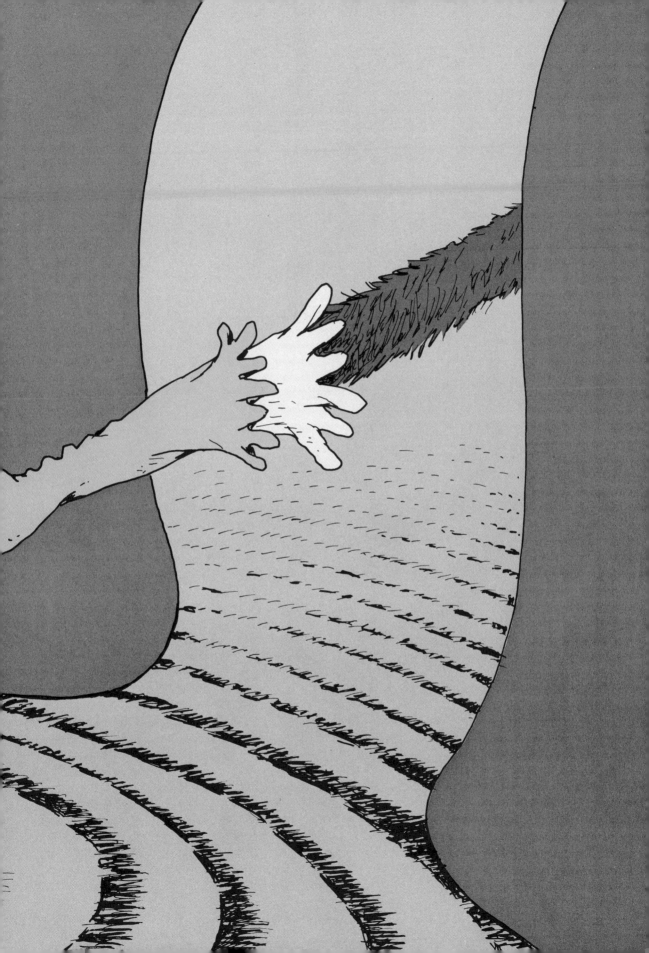

Then a Spookish Hunch suggested
I go four ways all at once!
But I didn't fall for *that* one.
I am not that dumb a dunce.

I knew where I would end up
if I tried a thing like *that*…

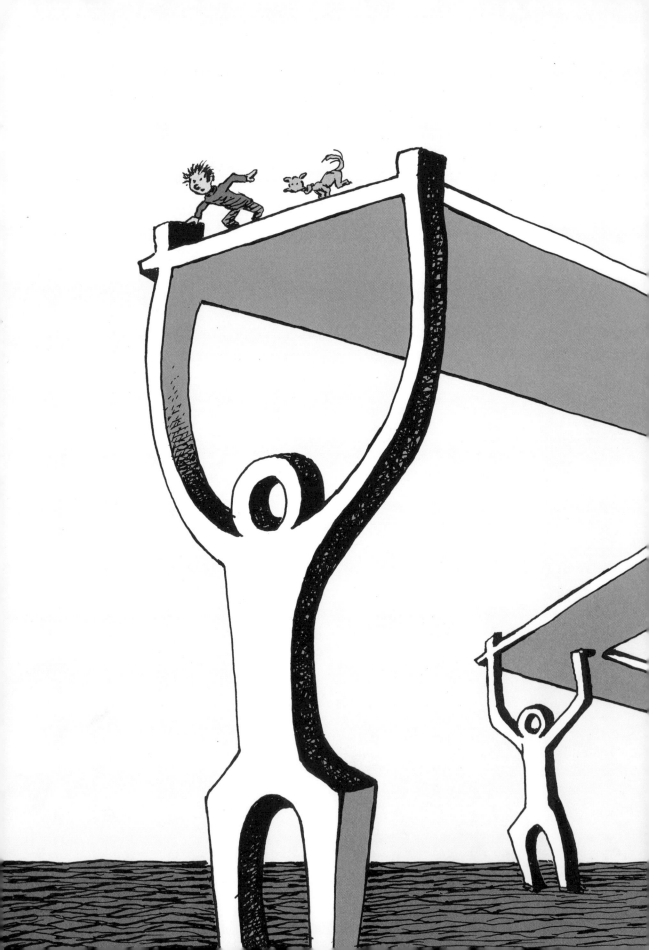

Most likely
on some dead-end road
in West Gee-Hossa-Flat!

I was much too smart
for that Four-Way Hunch.
But the next thing that I knew,
I was following a Nowhere Hunch,
a real dumb thing to do!

Everybody sometimes does it.
Even me. And even you.
I followed him in circles
till we wore the rug right through.

And then I heard
an Up Hunch laugh,
"You are a stupid schlupp!"

"The way to go
is not *around*.
The way to go
is UP!"

That seemed to make
a lot of sense.
I even took my chair.
I just knew
I'd make my mind up
if it had some high fresh air.

But the Up Hunch I had followed
was a phony and a fake!
Way up top I met a DOWN Hunch
and he sighed, "For goodness sake!
You should *never* trust an UP Hunch.
You have made a big mistake!"

Then things got really out of hand.
Wild hunches in big bunches
were scrapping all around me,
throwing crunchy hunchy punches.

And some Super Hunch was yelling,
"Make your mind up! Get it done!
Only *you* can make your mind up!
You're the one and only one!"

One of me
could *never* do it.
And quite suddenly I knew...

To get a job like that done
would take more of me
...like two!

And maybe
even more of me!

Like *three* of me!

Or four of me!

It took an awful lot of me.
It took a lot of yelling.
It took a lot of shoving
and hot bargaining and selling.

We all talked the hunches over,
up and down and through and through.
We argued and we barg-ued!
We decided what to do.

And I finally followed a Munch Hunch,
the best hunch of the bunch!
I followed him into the kitchen
and had six hot dogs for lunch.

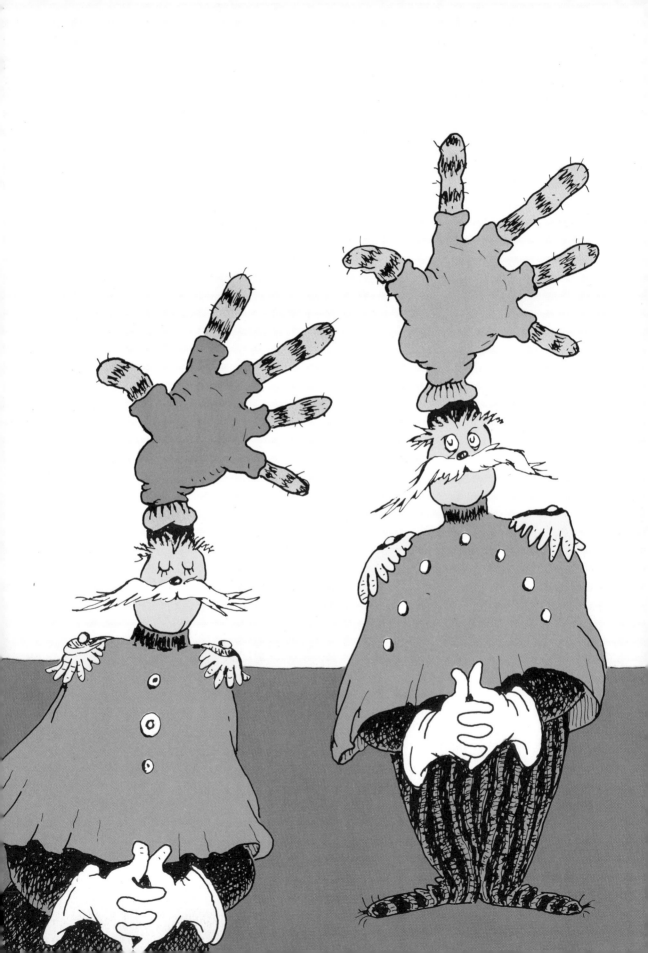

Lukeinrel